To
  Savannah & Dane~

With best wishes,

    Jane Aylott

The Soft Secret Word

by Jane Aylott

Original Paintings by Benny Andersson

To the True Family

Winged Peoples Press

It had been a good week.

"Actually, it was the best week of my life, " reflected God as he swung gently to and fro in the hammock he'd slung between two trees.

God's long-thought-of masterpiece was at last finished and the planet Earth in all her glory hung like a rich jewel in the dark cosmos.

As God lay snoozing in the warm sunshine, pleased and proud of all his magnificent creation, he suddenly had an idea. He got up and with a loud voice he summoned all the animals of the world, who came running to him from all directions, eagerly responding to their Creator's call.

"Now, everyone," announced God in a loud voice so that everyone could hear, only not so loud that he deafened the ants, "it gave me such joy to create you that I want to share some of my happiness by giving you all a blessing. Each one of you may have one wish and I will do my best to grant it."

The animals, understandably, were a little overawed by such an offer and hung back timidly.

"Come along now," said God encouragingly. "Don't be shy."

So Ostrich boldly stepped forward. Ostriches were a bit different in those days—more like extra large geese.

"Please, Sir," said Ostrich, taking a deep breath. "My wish is that I'd like to have lovely long legs, soft furry feathers, a swan-like neck, big eyes and fluttery eyelashes." She said it all in one breath and then blushed, embarrassed.

It was actually about five wishes, but God hadn't the heart to refuse her. So he spoke a soft secret word—and suddenly there she stood, exactly as she had pictured herself.

Not everyone thought Ostrich quite as glamorous as she did and Lion couldn't control a great roar of laughter. Frightened out of her wits, Ostrich found the nearest hole in the ground and thrust her head down it.

"What on earth are you doing?" asked Tiger incredulously.

"Hiding," came the muffled voice of Ostrich.

At which, of course, the whole assembly burst into gales of laughter.

"Oh dear," muttered God, half apologetically. "Well, she didn't leave me much room for a brain."

Next to come forward was Fox. It wasn't an ordinary kind of fox, but the smaller variety that lives in trees in Africa.

"Please, Sir," said Fox in a small but clear voice. "I wish I could be a bird."

This one had God stumped for a moment.

"Well, I can't actually change you into something else now that I've created you...." he began, and then he saw the look of disappointment come over Fox's face. "Er... but... um... I know! How about if I fitted you with a nice pair of wings?"

Fox was overjoyed. Then God spoke a soft secret word and Fox began to change. His fingers grew out long and spindly and between his fingers and his feet and all down each side there grew a piece of fine skin which stretched wide when he jumped and caught the air beneath it. It looked a bit like Bat's wing.

Fox squealed with delight and was off at once, leaping and sailing from treetop to treetop, and forever more he was known as Flying Fox.

God was really enjoying himself.

"Come along! Who's next? There are lots of blessings left yet!"

So one by one the animals came forward, each choosing something very special that he wanted. God made a lot of dreams come true that day.

Towards the end of the afternoon, it was Skunk's turn to choose. She came forward in her beautiful black and white coat and was so shy that you could hardly hear her.

"Please, Sir, I would like to be so fierce and ferocious that all the other animals would run away when they saw me."

"What an extraordinary ambition!" cried Tiger, which sounded a bit odd coming from so fierce an animal as he.

"Oh, Skunk," sighed God. "I'm right out of ferocious blessings. I've given tusks to Elephant, sharp teeth to Lion, big claws to Bear—I don't think I've got anything fierce left." It nearly broke his heart to see Skunk's eyes fill with tears of disappointment. God racked and racked his brain.

"I have it!" he cried, clapping his hands. "Come here, Skunk, and I'll whisper."

Skunk listened to God and a big beaming smile spread from ear to ear. Then

God whispered a soft secret word and said: "Go on now. Show them!"

Skunk went up on her forepaws in a magnificent handstand and at the same time ejected a stream of pale liquid.

The animals scattered as one, howling, roaring, screeching their dismay.

"Pooh, what a ghastly smell!" squeaked Marmoset from a safe distance.

"It's a most horrendous effluvium!" boomed Elephant, who can be forgiven for using big words, as he had, after all, had a somewhat larger whiff than most.

Skunk, naturally, was thrilled to bits.

The very last of all to come before God was Man. The other animals all felt sorry for Man and sad that he only had one wish.

"He's bound to wish for a fur coat," thought Mink and Ermine.

"He'll choose a tail," thought Peacock.

"Look at those feet," muttered Duck with pity in her voice.

Many animals wondered why God had bothered to create Man at all.

Man stood erect and proud before God but spoke out his request with humility.

"Please, Father, I wish to be like you. I want to learn to love."

There was a stunned silence and then all the animals began talking at once.

"Did you hear that?... of all the cheek... the impudent stripling... Man dared to call Sir FATHER...."

The animals were all deeply shocked, but God... God himself was so moved that he had to swallow about six times before he could speak.

"Oh, my dearest child," he said, embracing Man. "How dearly I have longed for this! And that you should choose it of your own desiring makes me glad beyond measure.

"But it is a hard path you have chosen. Will you be brave and kind and eager and sincere? Will you dare to give all of your heart where it is most shunned? Will you be able to bear the pain of too much tenderness?"

"I will," replied Man without hesitation, and he placed his hand confidently in God's.

Published by Winged Peoples Press
40 Hillside Avenue
Succasunna, New Jersey 07876

Library of Congress Cataloging in Publication Data

Aylott, Jane
The Soft Secret Word
Story by Jane Aylott
Original paintings by Benny Andersson

Summary: Overjoyed at finishing his Creation, God decides
to grant the wish of any creature, and is surprised
at the response he gets.

ISBN 0-9631440-0-6

The art for each picture is an original acrylic painting,
which is color-separated and reproduced in full color.